To the memory of my editor and friend,

JEAN KARL

BEAUTIFUL BLACKBIRD

BEAUTIFUL
BLACKBIRD

Ashley Bryan

Atheneum Books for Young Readers
New York London Toronto Sydney Singapore

A long, long time ago, the birds of Africa were all colors of the rainbow . . . clean, clear colors from head to tail. Oh so pretty, pretty, pretty!

Back then, though, birds had no marks of black on their feathers. From the tops of their heads to the tips of their tails, no markings of black, uh-uh! Whether large or small, Blackbird was the only bird who had it all.

One day Ringdove called the birds to a festival in the forest. He asked them all to meet by the lake where he lived.

Birds flew in from all over. With a flip-flop-flapping of their wings and a whirring, stirring of the air, they flew down to the lake from everywhere.

The birds' colors were mirrored in the waters.

They were red, green, yellow, purple, orange, and blue, pink, then black, black, Blackbird, uh-huh, Blackbird, too.

Ringdove called, "Coo-coo-roo,
coo-ca-roo, I've a question to ask of you.
Who of all is the most beautiful?"
  The colored birds never even raised
a wing. They raised their beaks and began
to sing,

"Blackbird stands out best of all.
Blackbird is the most beautiful.
His feathers gleam all colors in the sun.
Blackbird is the most beautiful one."

The birds circled Blackbird in a Beak and
Wing Dance, singing,

"Beak to beak, peck, peck, peck,
Spread your wings, stretch your neck.
Black is beautiful, uh-huh!
Black is beautiful, uh-huh!"

They broke out of the circle for the Show Claws Slide,

"Tip tap toe to the left, spin around,
Toe tap tip to the right, stroke the ground.
Wings flip-flapping as you glide,
Forward and backward in a Show Claws Slide."

When the birds were into their steps, Ringdove took Blackbird aside. "Oh Blackbird, Blackbird, coo-coo-roo, coo-ca-roo, would you color me black so that I'll be black like you? My neck is plain and that's a shame, 'cause Ringdove is my given name."

Blackbird said, "Color on   the outside is not what's on the inside.
You don't act like me. You don't eat like me. You don't get down in the groove
and move your feet like me. But come tomorrow to the Sun-Up Dance. I'll
brew some blackening in my medicine gourd. Then I'll swing a ring around
your neck to go with your name."

The next day the birds gathered. Blackbird stirred the blackening brew in his medicine gourd. He stirred it round and round.

Then he dipped his feather brush into the pot. With his free wing he spun Ringdove around, holding his brush to Ringdove's neck.

Ringdove sang, "Coo-coo-roo, Coo-ca-roo!
See what a swinging ring of black can do!"

Blackbird bowed to the crowd as a chirping arose,

"Ringdove's black is beautiful.
Beak to beak, peck, peck, peck,
He's just like Blackbird
Around the neck."

"Oh Blackbird, can we have some of that blackening too?
We all need what your black can do.
You're such an artist with your feather brush,
A touch of your black will be good for us."
Blackbird said, "Tomorrow, I'll mix the rest of my black roots in a
larger medicine gourd. I'll give what I can give until it all gives out."

The birds danced the Sun-Down
Dance, then went to nest. All through the
night the birds dreamed of black.

Black markings on the head,
Tail, wing, front, or back.
Oh, black is beautiful
Black, black, black.

Birds rose at sun up and took to their wings. Oh, way up high, their colors filled the sky. With a flip-flop-flapping of their wings, a stirring, whirring of the air, they flew down to the lake from everywhere. Ringdove carried Blackbird's large gourd and set it down.

Blackbird stirred with a stick in his wing and said, "We'll see the difference a touch of black can make. Just remember, whatever I do, I'll be me and you'll be you."

Blackbird tipped his feather brush into the pot and tapped out dots. Some were large. Some were small. Close together or far apart, it was a challenge to Blackbird's art.

With strokes long and short he painted stripes. Blackbird swept his brush strokes steady. He drew lines only when his brush was ready and full with the black, black brew.

The paint in the gourd was getting low. Blackbird still had more to go before he had decorated the birds with black, one and all.

"Save some for us!" cried the small birds. "We've been in line and we were on time. We won't step back till we get a touch of black, too, uh-huh, uh-huh!"

Ringdove tipped the gourd. Blackbird slipped his brush way, way in. He brushed the rest of the birds with marks and arcs. He black-tapped the last small bird of the flock.

Then Blackbird sang,
"I've painted plenty, plenty, plenty,
The gourd's now empty, empty, empty."

The birds surrounded Blackbird and sang,

"Our colors sport a brand-new look,
A touch of black was all it took.
Oh beautiful black, uh-huh, uh-huh
Black is beautiful, UH-HUH!"

AUTHOR'S NOTE: The scissors shown on the endpapers are the scissors
that my mother used in her sewing and embroidery and that I, in turn,
used in cutting the paper for the collages in this book.

Atheneum Books for Young Readers

An imprint of Simon & Schuster Children's Publishing Division

1230 Avenue of the Americas

New York, New York 10020

Adapted from a tale from *The Ila-speaking Peoples from Northern Rhodesia* (now known as Zambia)

by Edwin W. Smith and Andrew M. Dale. University Books: New Hyde Park, New York, 1968. vol. 2, pp. 350–51.

Book design by Abelardo Martínez

The text of this book is set in Matrix.

The illustrations are rendered in paper collage.

Manufactured in China

2 4 6 8 10 9 7 5 3

Bryan, Ashley.

Beautiful blackbird / Ashley Bryan—1st ed.

p.   cm.

Summary: In a story of the Ila people, the colorful birds of Africa ask Blackbird, whom they think is the most beautiful of birds,

to decorate them with some of his "blackening brew."

ISBN 0-689-84731-9

[1. Ila (African people)—Folklore. 2. Folklore—Zambia.]

PZ8.1+

398.2 E 21   2002005290